# Taking Care of Crumley

To my parents

Kids Can Press gratefully acknowledges
the assistance of the Canada Council
and the Ontario Arts Council
in the production of this book.

Canadian Cataloguing in Publication Data
Staunton, Ted, 1956
Taking care of Crumley
ISBN 0-919964-75-3 (bound)
ISBN 0-919964-55-9 (pbk)

I. Holdcroft, Tina    II. Title.
PS8587.T38T34    1984        jC813′.54        C84-098731-5
PZ7.S72Ta    1984

Kids Can Press,
585½ Bloor Street West,
Toronto, Ontario, Canada, M6G 1K5.

Book design by Wycliffe Smith
Printed by Everbest Printing Co., Ltd. Hong Kong.

# Taking Care of Crumley

*Written by Ted Staunton*
*Illustrated by Tina Holdcroft*

**KIDS CAN PRESS, TORONTO**

When it all began, I was hanging upside down.
Suddenly the jungle gym shook.
It got dark all around and I was looking at
Ugly Augie Crumley and his Goons —
the biggest bullies in school. Was I ever scared!

Ugly Augie smiled. He liked to scare kids.
He pushed me, pinched me, poked me, pulled
my ears, and just plain picked on me.
Then they left me with my shoes tied to the bars
and a promise to pick on me a whole lot more.

As soon as I got free, I went to see Maggie,
the Greenapple Street genius.
"Can you make Ugly Augie stop bugging me?"
I asked. Maggie laughed. "No problem, Cyril.
But … you'll have to do anything I say."
"No way!" I said. Then I remembered Ugly Augie's
promise. "Okay," I sighed.
"Good," said Maggie. "Tomorrow I'll take care of
Crumley. This is going to be fun!"

The next day was Friday. Maggie came down Greenapple Street and told me a Perfectly Perfect Plan. I had to tell a lie to Ugly Augie without anyone else hearing.

When I got to school, I snuck up to Ugly Augie and whispered, "Crumley, you're going to get it!" It felt nice to say.

A little louder I said, "My cousin Vern, who is in Grade 7 and plays football, is coming after school to make you into mush with one hand!" That felt even nicer.

I shouted, "He'll make you look like a hockey puck!"
Then I roared, "You're all washed up, bozo!"
and walked away like a big hero.

Maggie said that Ugly Augie was just a bully
who was chicken inside. After school he would
run home so fast that he'd never know I didn't have
a cousin Vern. I thought my problem was solved.

Sure enough, after school I saw Ugly Augie
sneaking off for home. Then I heard the Goons.
"Hey Augie, where are you going?"
"You can beat this guy!"
Now I knew why I was supposed to whisper —
to keep the Goons away.
I got scared all over again. They came around
the corner and saw me — all alone. I gulped.
They charged, and I ran for my life.

Suddenly there was Maggie on her bike.
"Hop on," she shouted, and we took off.
"You're gonna pay for lying to me, Cyril,"
yelled Ugly Augie.
"Bring us money on Monday or else!"

I told Maggie, "I forgot to whisper." She moaned.
"My best plan ever and you blew it, Cyril.
Now I have to start all over, and you have to
carry my books. And watch out for the poison
ivy around here."
We went home to Greenapple Street and didn't
say another word.

I worried all weekend while Maggie sat in her tree
thinking. At last, on Sunday, she came down.
She was dressed very strangely.
"Cyril," she said, "I have a Terribly Terrific Plan.
Open your piggy bank and put all your pennies
in this bag."
When I was done, she took the bag and headed
down the street.
"See you tomorrow," was all she said.

Monday morning Maggie was ready.

"Here's the plan," she said.

"Tell Ugly Augie you have poison ivy.
Then try to give him the bag of pennies.
He'll be scared to touch you or your
money ever again."

"Not another lie," I groaned. "I don't even
have poison ivy."

"No, dummy," said Maggie, "but I'll
make you look like you do."

When she was finished, Maggie smiled.

"You sure look sick," she said.

"Now go do your stuff."

I started to walk, but my knees were knocking.
Every penny I owned was in that bag.
What if I didn't fool them?
I peeked around the corner. Ugly Augie looked
awfully ugly that morning. The Goons looked like
grumpy gorillas. I got goose bumps all over.

I opened the bag and stuffed some money
in my shirt, just in case. Then I walked
out to the jungle gym.

Slowly they circled me.

My stomach got all squishy.

Ugly Augie smiled and said, "Gimme."

"H-h-here," I said. "But I have poison ivy
and if you touch me or my stuff you'll get it too!"

Ugly Augie stared. Then he rubbed my face.

"Lipstick," he snorted. "This kid always lies."

He snatched my money and in a second
they all had some.

The Terribly Terrific Plan had turned
terrifically terrible.

But when I ran back to Maggie and told her
what had happened, she began to laugh.
"It worked, it worked," she whooped.
"I knew they'd take the money!"
"What?" I said.
"Yesterday I took your pennies to the field and
mushed them up with poison ivy," she said.
"Augie and his Goons are going to itch like crazy.
And they'll be scared to touch you in case they
get even more. I've taken care of Crumley!"

"All right!" I roared, and we danced around.
After a minute, I stopped. I felt itchy.
Maggie scratched her hands. Then I remembered.
"Oh, no," I said. Slowly I felt inside my shirt.
"I kept some of the money," I whispered.
"Eeeek," screeched Maggie. "You dummy.
We have poison ivy!"

We itched for a month. Everybody got in trouble
for what they did to everybody else, and
everybody blamed me.

One day I met Ugly Augie on Greenapple Street.
"Oh, oh," I thought, but he ran away.
"You keep away from me, Cyril," he yelled.
I went to the schoolyard. A couple of the Goons
were there, but they hid when they saw me.
"Quit picking on us, Cyril," they shouted.
Suddenly everything was all right. Maggie's plan
had worked. Ugly Augie had stopped bugging me.
We had taken care of Crumley!